THEN, THEY WERE CROWS

JENNI WARD

MIRAWORTH BOOKS

First published in 2024
by Miraworth Books
ABN 44 964 848 123

MIRAWORTH BOOKS
PO Box 3523, Mount Gambier, SA 5290, Australia

ISBN (e-book): 978-0-6453270-9-0
ISBN (paperback): 978-0-6458856-2-0

Cover by Miraworth Designs

A catalogue record for this book is available from the National Library of Australia

Please note this book is written in Australian English.
Grammar and spelling differs from US English.

Dreams may be a window to our innermost thoughts, but they also hold the key to our future, revealing glimpses of what is yet to come

A young woman in a simple dark blue dress stepped barefoot across the dirt. Above, the sky blanketed the scene; dark, cold, jet-black, and not a star to be found. She paused to cast her gaze over her surroundings.

Her fingers tightly gripped the fabric of her skirt. It flared as she turned around. Her gaze taking in where she stood: the centre of the village square. All around her, half-timbered buildings with steeply pitched roofs rose up. The paint on the buildings, faded and peeled away in places, revealed the rough-hewn beams that were once hidden away.

Beneath her feet, the smooth cobblestone streets were free of weeds and grass. A few fallen leaves play in the breeze nearby, drawing her attention for a moment.

Despite the lack of people, the lamps that hung outside of the shops and houses continued to burn as if at any moment the square would be full of chatter again. A feeling of emptiness overwhelmed her as the lit lamps cast their glow over the shadows.

"Hello?" her voice trembled as she spoke.

She took a small step forward. Her legs shook and threatened to collapse under her weight.

"Mother?" Her head whipped to the left, only to be met with emptiness. "Father?"

A breeze played with the girl's shoulder length black hair. She waited for any response: a bird chirping, a branch falling, soft footsteps from another...but the silence continued. Her feet shuffled as she turned again, before she wrapped her arms around herself in a hug.

A noise to the left. Her body shook as she focused in that direction. Unusual noises echoed from the narrow lane that separated two of the buildings. Something moved in the shadows. Her breathing quickened.

"He...Hello?" her voice wavered. "It's just the shadows. The shadows and the light from the lamps playing tricks."

Her feet took small steps towards the fountain nearby. The stone stood tall with its surface carved with intricate designs of wolves in various poses. Each wolf depicted in great detail, so they appeared to be guarding the water, their piercing eyes gazing out from the stone. No water flowed from the top of the fountain to the carved basin below. The water sat still, with a handful of black feathers resting on the surface.

The girl turned and fled from the town. Her feet pounded the dirt road as she hurried towards distant lights. She ran and ran. Ran until another village stood before her. Her gaze barely took in the name of the village on the wooden sign next to the road.

Cobblestones replaced the dirt beneath her feet. The houses on either side were adorned with colourful banners, streamers, and flowers. She focused on the village square ahead, the air filled with the sound of music, laughter, and chatter.

Snowflakes began to fall. She continued to run, but when she reached the square, the flames in the lamps went out. The air turned icy. The sky went dark. People around her stood still.

Loud cawing echoed through the air. The girl looked skyward as the sleek black bodies, with wings outstretched, glided towards the people. Their sharp beaks were slightly open. Intelligent eyes assessed the scene as they circled once, twice, three times.

Then the crows descended. As their flight pattern became chaotic and frenzied, the birds swooped and dove in all directions before their movements once again became synchronised.

A scream pierced the scene. People ran in all directions. The girl turned to find safety, but the crows crashed through windows, flew under wagons. They did whatever was needed to find the humans. She looked down as a crow pecked at the hem of her skirt.

"Shoo, get away!" she yelled.

The words didn't deter the bird. Soon, a dozen birds pulled on the fabric and the girl fell to the ground under a flurry of black feathers. The crows continued to caw and chatter amongst themselves, their voices rose in a raucous chorus.

My eyelids opened, no doubt revealing bloodshot eyes. Bleak darkness faded, replaced by the familiar walls of my room. I rubbed at the grit, hoping to erase the dream. Dreams. So many people dreamt at night, some even had nightmares, but theirs were products of their imaginations. For me, a vivid dream was never just a dream.

The day called. I tossed the blankets away, my feet hitting the warm floorboards. Despite the gloomy skies outside, the room kept the heat from the fire that had burned through the night. I pushed myself off the bed and walked toward the window, snagging my hairbrush on the way. As I worked the brush through my long, wavy auburn hair, I contemplated the dream.

"Was there snow?" I mumbled. "We haven't had snow here yet, but they have nearer the city; the newspaper reported it last week."

News from the big city always arrived late. We only received one newspaper a month, and the events reported were already

9

weeks old. Still, if snow had fallen there, it wouldn't be long before the little villages around Snowrush Forest would be cut off. Until then, I wanted to enjoy walking without the thick boots and coats required during deep winter.

Free of knots, I grabbed a ribbon and plaited my hair, knowing it wouldn't last long. Strands always seemed to work their way free. In seventeen years, I still found managing my hair a challenge, but I didn't dare cut it. My mother loved seeing it long, telling me each year on my birthday how much it reminded her of my father, who passed away before I turned eight.

I grabbed my blue dress from a hanger near the window and slipped it on. I'd read how city society expected four layers of fabric on young ladies at all times, but in the villages, nobody commented if a girl decided to forgo them. It was more practical, after all.

Dressed and awake, I left the comfort of my bedroom and stepped onto the landing. The scent of cedar wood surrounded me as I trailed my hand on the railing while descending the stairs.

As usual, I could hear my mother humming in the kitchen. I peeked around the door frame. She had just plated toast with a fried egg on top. There was no slipping out unnoticed. After a deep breath, I plastered a smile on my face and entered.

My mother looked up and smiled. As I sat, she picked up the plates and brought them to the table. Food in front of me, I wasted no time eating. It was an effective way to avoid answering questions.

"Any dreams last night?" my mother asked.

"Not really," I mumbled around a mouthful of toast.

I wiped my mouth on the back of my sleeve. Beneath the table, my hand tapped nervously against my leg. My gaze moved from the empty plate to the door and back again.

"What does that mean?"

"I mean, I slept, but didn't dream of anything you need to know about."

I looked up to see her face set. An awkward laugh escaped my lips, and her stare intensified.

"Larissa, honey, is something wrong?"

"No, nothing's wrong. I just…" I searched for a believable excuse. "Woke up on the wrong side of the bed."

Her eyebrows rose. I stared at my empty plate.

"Alright, as long as you are–"

The chair scraped on the wooden floor as I stood.

"I promised to meet someone this morning. See you after I pick up your things," I said, grabbing the list she had written the night before from the table next to the front door. She stood, but I was already out the door before she could finish her sentence.

Down the road, I slowed to a walk. I'd glanced behind several times, but my mother wasn't following. At ease, my pace slackened.

"Good morning, Larissa!"

I raised my gaze to see my elderly neighbour in her garden, rounding up some cats darting around her legs. I waved but continued towards the village square.

"What if it was a future dream?" I whispered.

This was what I disliked most. If it was a present dream, I knew I'd be too late to stop whatever I saw, but if it was a future dream, I felt the need to warn the village. But first, I needed to work out the name of the first village in my dream.

"Larissa, could you come over here? There's something I wanted to talk to you about." The familiar voice was unmistakable.

Abandoning my thoughts, I walked toward Barkley as he organised the rolls of bread at the front of his shop. The warm aroma of freshly baked goods beckoned me closer. My gaze moved from the rolls to the shelves behind him, where an array of pastries and cakes were arranged neatly on the wooden shelves.

Barkley's round face lit up as I stopped before him. I'd known him since I was little. Back then, he'd been an apprentice baker, but now he owned the shop.

"Did you hear the news? You couldn't have been more spot on. I proposed just the way you said it would happen… and Sally said yes! Thank you, Larissa."

"You didn't need my help. I'm sure she would have said yes, however you proposed," I replied. I firmly believed that to be true.

"Maybe, maybe. Sally has been busy preparing for a spring wedding. If you get any dreams about it—let me know. I want the perfect day for her."

I nodded, even though I had no control over my dreams. I turned to continue toward the tea shop when Mrs. Carew bustled over. If anyone had a secret in town, it was her.

"Did you hear about the village two over?" She directed it to Barkley. "Word came this morning from one of the wagon sellers. The entire place is empty. Not a soul to be found, and no clues where they disappeared to."

"How strange," Barkley replied.

Mrs. Carew turned to me and narrowed her gaze. "You wouldn't know anything about that, would you?"

I hesitated. "I don't…I don't think so," I replied.

"Think? Hmm, maybe one of your dreams showed something amiss?"

I squirmed under her unrelenting gaze.

"I saw it empty, nothing else." The words tumbled out before I could stop them. I'd kept it from my mother, but now...

Mrs. Carew turned to Barkley. "If you ask me, those dreams of hers are rubbish or the work of evil."

With a curt nod to Barkley, completely ignoring me, she walked away.

"Don't mind what she says. We both know your dreams are something special," Barkley reassured me.

A voice from inside the shop called him away.

Alone again, I continued toward the tea shop. It wouldn't be open just yet, but I knew my friend Katie would be out back, preparing. Two small tables, each with two chairs, sat at the front. The sign on the door still hung with 'closed.'

I followed the edge of the building down the narrow lane between the tea shop and the dressmaker. My finger flicked the metal clasp on the closed wooden gate, and it swung open without a creak.

I spotted Katie through the open back door. We'd known each other since our first year of school, when her family moved to the village after buying the building that was now the tea rooms.

Her brown hair was pinned in a bun under a partly see-through white cap. She wore a pale blue blouse with a high collar and a long, dark blue skirt, but a crisp white apron obscured both. She stood at a large wooden table, preparing cake slices, and raised her head as I entered.

"You're a bit early. I won't be on break for at least another half hour," she said.

"I wanted to ask you something. Because, you know, you've seen so much of this area," I replied.

"Better make it quick. If Mama hears us, I'll get extra duties for the day."

"Do you know of a village nearby that has a fountain with wolves on it?" I asked, stepping further inside the room to keep my voice low.

Katie placed two more cakes on the plate before she looked up.

"The only one I know of is over at Larks Crossing. It's a couple of villages over, but not more than a day on foot." She rested her hand on mine. "Is this about what happened there? The missing people?"

"I saw something, but I don't know that I understand it. What would be the next closest villages?"

"There are a couple. I went last year with Papa to Mossmead. Large village with the best animal shop I've ever seen. They have these fancy banners on the buildings and these colourful little flags all around the town square. So pretty."

She turned and grabbed two more plates.

"There's Willowmist Pass as well. That's a little closer than Mossmead. My uncle doesn't enjoy getting work in Willowmist. They insist on doing stuff the old way." Katie moved the completed plate to the bench and started on a new one. "They must be the only village that still has a wooden sign at the entrance. My uncle offered to build them a stone one. All they had to do was pay for the stone, and he'd work for free, but no. They're so traditional."

"Any others?" I asked. I already had the answer I needed, but didn't want my mother to find out. It would make it easy to bring me back if I went to Willowmist.

"There's Grange, that's a little further over that way." She pointed to the back of the shop. "And there's–"

"Katie, have you finished those plates?" a chirpy voice interrupted.

"Quick, go," Katie hissed.

I pressed myself against the gate just as hard-soled shoes marched into the room.

"Hurry up. We still need to finish the drinks," Katie's mother said.

As soon as the shoes departed, I slipped out the gate. I had the money for the things my mother wanted, but I needed a few supplies of my own.

"I'll have enough left over. I'll just make sure I'm back by the afternoon."

With enough supplies tucked into a small bag, I set out for Willowmist Pass. Hours passed. As I trudged along the hardened ground, the air chilled. I'd never walked to another village before. Usually, I sat in the back of a wagon, chatting away with others.

"Walking takes forever," I grumbled, my feet aching.

Ahead, a branch lay across the dirt road. I reached it and slumped to the ground beside it. My eyelids felt heavy, and my side ached. I lacked the motivation to pull anything from the bag for a snack, choosing instead to take advantage of the old oak. Its branches, except for the fallen one, stretched over the road, providing a canopy against the elements.

I pulled my shawl tight against my shoulders, shivering despite the exertion of the walk. As my body accepted the pause, spasms ran up my legs.

"Just a little rest," I whispered, "and I'll make it through."

I rested my head against the rough wood of the branch and closed my eyes.

Caw…

My eyes flew open, still tired but alert. There was no sign of the crow, and it didn't call again. I scanned the trees and the sky, then stood up, uneasiness prickling my skin.

"If you're going to attack me," I said, my voice trembling slightly, "I'll stand and fight."

Not that I'd ever raised a hand to anyone or anything before. Still, the landscape betrayed nothing that might be concealed.

I grabbed my bag and moved swiftly down the road. While Katie's uncle might not have liked the Willowmist Pass sign, for me, it was a welcome sight after that eerie encounter. Especially as night had arrived.

"Mum is going to be so upset with me," I murmured.

My pace slowed as the dirt road became cobblestones. The buildings stood with their doors closed, but curtains were open in the windows despite the darkness. I recognised the colourful banners, streamers, and flowers from my dream. But no music played.

"I'm too late," I whispered. "The people are already gone."

My footsteps echoed in the empty streets as I ventured deeper into the village. Black feathers lay on the cobblestones, almost like they were leading me to the square. When it came into view, my shoulders slumped.

"Maybe if I look around a little more," I mumbled, "I might find some clues. Something I didn't see in my dream." I paused, gazing at the empty square. "Where do I start?"

I pulled the shawl around my shoulders, knowing I wouldn't make it home tonight. Finding a suitable place to stay was a top priority.

"Mother will be so worried," I mused, walking past the empty buildings.

Meow.

Finally, a sound of life. I turned, listening for the tiny cries. My gaze focused on the steps leading up to one building.

Meow.

A deep chill ran through me as light, fluffy snowflakes fell, catching on my long, wavy hair. I raised my face toward the cloudy sky and saw a single crow flying high above.

"Perhaps you're searching for the kitten too," I said. "Though a meal is more likely on your mind than making a friend." The crow disappeared from view.

Meow.

I glanced down. A tiny grey kitten huddled at my feet. It

rubbed its face against my boots before looking up at me, eyes wide.

"Oh, you poor little thing," I murmured, scooping it into my hands. I held the shivering creature close to my body. "We need to find some shelter."

I felt bad about entering someone else's house, but I hoped they would forgive me if I could ever find them.

More snowflakes fell, and I started walking toward one building to my right: the library. When I reached the door, the handle turned without objection. The door swung open silently, revealing tables, chairs, and shelves of books.

I closed the door firmly behind me and kicked the draught blocker into place. Rubbing my arms for warmth, I glanced around, searching for something to light. I didn't want to be trapped in a dark library alone if the snow turned into something more than a light sprinkling.

I dropped my bag on the floor. The room was still warm, making the village's abandonment all the more unsettling.

"If the people of Willowmist have been turned into crows, where are they now?" I muttered to the kitten. "I need to find them, and fast."

The little cat didn't reply, too busy nudging at my bag. Outside, the wind beat against the window panes in short bursts. I eyed the wooden shutters, knowing I could close them if the weather worsened.

"It's still warm," I said. "It's silly because I noticed it wasn't as cold in here when I walked in, but it's warm, like someone just put the fire out."

The fireplace was empty, but the smell of burnt wood lingered.

"With any luck, kitty," I said, "the village has only just been abandoned. Maybe I arrived within minutes of them disappearing."

The kitten swiped at the bag's handle before tumbling head over paws as she attacked it. I smiled.

I took off my shawl and placed it over the back of a chair. Enough snowflakes had caught on the fabric that wet patches darkened the patterns, but I had no time to fuss over it. I needed light before the night darkened the room.

My gaze swept over tables and bookshelves as I turned on the spot. The villagers, who often paid to bring them in from the cities far away, highly valued books. The librarians had to ensure they remained in good condition, and fire remained the biggest threat to the pages.

"Still, the librarian would have had some way to light the room even with the dangers," I mumbled.

The librarian's desk sat to one side near a wall. There were no windows on that side, and the shelves reached no higher than my waist. Instead, the wood panels of the wall featured a painting.

The subdued colours hinted at either the age of the work or the artist's fondness for avoiding vibrant colours. A lady stood tall and poised, with a serene expression. Her attire comprised a flowing dress and a bonnet that reminded me of the distant past. Her delicate features were accentuated by her calm expression, and her gaze fixed on the pages of the book she held open in her hand.

"You think she was someone from the village?" I asked the kitten. "A rich lady who donated to the library, perhaps?"

I turned away from the painting and focused on the desk. I walked over and reached for the handle of the top drawer. It slid open with a soft rumble, revealing pieces of paper and pencils. The second drawer held more papers, these filled with a log of names, books, and dates.

"There must be some way to light it in here," I muttered. No reply.

I opened the third drawer. This one was deeper and contained exactly what I wanted: a candle in a holder and matches. Just as the room was becoming difficult to see in, I struck a match, and a flame came to life on the candle. I gave the flame time to settle, not wanting a sudden movement to send the room back into darkness.

With the candle in one hand, matches in the other, I walked to the fireplace and crouched down. There were a few logs beside it, and I placed them on the burnt ones. The flame danced as I placed it on the ground, stirring the kitten's curiosity.

"I'll need something to light it." I stood up. "You be careful with that flame, kitty."

I watched the kitten sniff at the flame, but she didn't move closer. I hurried back to the desk and opened the top drawer to retrieve a handful of paper sheets. They made lighting the logs much easier. Soon, the waning warmth returned to a comforting temperature.

I settled into a large comfy chair near the fire. While the wind howled outside, I pulled my feet up onto the chair, my skirt hiding them from view. I reached for the books that sat on the small table beside the chair. The first one didn't interest me, but the second—a book of children's stories—I opened.

My eyelids felt heavy, though, and the words blurred as I read. I felt the plop of a tiny body on my legs before the kitten circled until she found a spot that suited her. Soon, both of us were asleep.

When confronted with an unknown evil,
courage and caution must walk hand in hand, for only then
can we hope to unveil its true nature and overcome it.

Laughter echoed around Larissa. She opened her eyes. Her gaze found she was alone and yet the laughter must have come from someone.

It came again, playing with the breeze. Larissa turned to find the source of the childlike sound, but as she searched, the lithe tone evolved into a sinister cackle. She froze as chills ran over Larissa's skin.

The village looked familiar…and yet…Larissa raised her hands. When she experienced her dreams, it had always been like watching others play their role. Much like the summer plays that were meant to teach children to be good.

"How is it I am me?" she whispered.

A gust of air. Larissa's hair whipped around her face as she fought to tame it with her hands. In the area before her, a black figure appeared. Hunched over but male, that much Larissa knew. He raised his head and stared at her with empty black eyes.

Black eyes, who has eyes like that? He smiled. Larissa's fingers tightened into a grip. *Can he read my thoughts?*

"Who—who are you?"

"Looks like I missed one," he replied.

His voice echoed around her as the raindrops hit against the cobblestones. Her clothes became drenched, and the weight held her captive in place. Lightning lit the sky and thunder clapped in the distance as Larissa tried to remain focused on the man.

"What are you?" It seemed a more fitting question as her heart beat faster.

The man stood up. Tall and wearing all black except for the white collar at the base of his neck. Larissa thought the long-tailed black jacket and fitted pants reminiscent of the high fashion of the city, and yet something about it seemed unfashionable. He seemed young, perhaps only a handful of years older than herself, definitely younger than Barkley the baker.

"Who, what…They're all a little subjective, aren't they? Who are you? What are you? A human? A girl? My next victim?"

"Victim?" The word stuck in the back of her throat. "You are behind the abandoned villages."

"Been clearing them out for years. First time someone seems to have noticed me." He stepped closer. "I make things appear and disappear."

He paused in his approach and raised his hands up and hundreds of crows appeared to fly from the blackness of his clothing. They rose in a spiral formation before circling above. Their forms were only visible as the lighting cut through the sky.

Larissa approached the man this time; her limbs shook more and more with each step. She swallowed, though her mouth felt dry. The man raised his hand in her direction and pointed his index finger at her. She paused. Waited. Nothing changed. Larissa took another step and another; the gap only a few arm lengths away.

"Something isn't right," his voice echoed around her.

He shook his finger at Larissa several times. With each attempt, his face reddened and his brows furrowed.

"Answer my question," Larissa demanded, emboldened by his frustration. "Who are you!"

"Why won't you…" his words tapered off as he lowered his hand. He straightened his black jacket and glowered at the girl before him. "People call me the Soul Stealer; you would be wise to remember it."

"Soul Stealer," she repeated. "I've not heard of you."

He smiled again: a cruel, twisted smile.

"I do not aim to be known any longer; I have other goals in life." He stepped to the side, continuing to keep his gaze on Larissa. "You, you are something new for me as well. This isn't real and yet I should have complete control in my mind, yet you continue to stand before me."

"Whatever you are doing with the people, you must stop. Those people have families and provide–"

"Provide me with what I desire, provide me with what I need. Perhaps I need you. Something so unexpectant in my mind and yet I feel the aura around you. I sense you carry a burden, not that unlike mine."

"I have no burden."

"Oh, but you do. You may call it something different. A curse maybe? Or a blessing? We all carry a burden on our shoulders, but some of us have ones that are more unique."

"You don't know that."

"I know you are here when you shouldn't be. I know nothing happened when it should have. That tells me many things even if I don't understand the meaning."

He stretched his arms out wide and took several steps backwards.

"Until we cross paths again."

When his arms lowered, another hundred crows rose in his place, leaving nothing of the man behind. Only the rain remained.

My eyes opened to a dim room, but not darkness. The fire still burned, though the flames were less vibrant than before. The little cat stretched her paws into the fabric of my skirt before snuggling her head down, hiding her nose behind her paws.

"Who was that?" I murmured. My voice sounded raspy from sleep. "Soul Stealer?"

I carefully picked up the kitten and placed her on the warm seat, rubbing the back of my neck as I went to the fireplace to add another log.

"There's enough logs here for a couple of days if I don't use it all the time," I said. The flames licked at the log, rewarding me with more light.

The candle on the table had burned out, leaving only a mound of wax behind. At least it confirmed that I'd slept for some time. My stomach growled, demanding attention.

"Something to eat first."

I retrieved my bag and sat on a worn rug in front of the fireplace. The kitten landed softly beside me, nuzzling my hand.

"Guess you're hungry too. Let me see what you might like."

I found some dried meat, and the kitten snatched it from my hand without hesitation. A soft growl murmured through the room as she chewed, hiding under the chair. I settled for a bread roll; the meat had been intended for it, but the roll alone would suffice.

Hunger pangs satisfied, I retrieved a fresh candle from the bottom drawer of the librarian's desk. After swapping out the blob of wax for the new candle, I lit it.

"Soul Stealer," I whispered, my gaze sweeping over the shelves of books. "I've never heard of anyone called that in any stories I heard as a child. It would help if these books had some kind of word system. Guess that would be too easy, huh, kitty?"

The kitten, content with the meat in her tummy, had no time for questions. She batted at a loose string under the chair before tackling it with both paws.

"I guess a library is the place to be trapped if I want to find something," I said. "He seemed to change shape from a crow, or crows really, to human… and probably vice versa. A section on mythological creatures makes sense."

I walked beside the shelves, looking for the section I needed. The organisation of this library differed from the one in my village, but I eventually found the books I wanted tucked away along a wall with no windows.

"Now, which ones to start with?"

I chose the thick encyclopaedia and another older book and returned to the chair. At least these books were organised the same way as all the others. I turned to the back to search the index. My finger slid down the page of creatures, but there was no Soul Stealer. I tried crows and transformation, but the closest I found was a myth from the far east of the kingdom about people returning as crows to seek revenge. It didn't quite fit the man I'd seen, but I slipped a bookmark into the page just in case.

Pages flipped past, stopping mid-flip when a word caught my eye. I breathed a sigh of relief that the librarian hadn't witnessed the rough handling of her books.

"Dreamers. Is that what I am?"

The kitten, having lost her battle with the loose string, hopped up beside me on the chair. She licked her paws before snuggling down for another nap.

"Dreamers are humans with the ability to receive insight when they sleep," I read aloud. "This rare occurrence allows the receiver to observe past, present, and future events. While younger dreamers struggle to control the frequency and type of dreams they receive, with time, many learn to focus their dreams on specific places, people, or events." I paused. "Well, that's all very easy to write, but I've never seen the past. At least, not that I know of."

It hadn't occurred to me that some of my dreams might have been in the past. If so, which ones?

"Could any of my dreams have been from before?" I mused. "Not very helpful. A list of people with the ability would be nice. Then at least I might know how they slept seeing nothing other than what their imaginations decided on."

Still, I slipped a second bookmark into the book.

It took some time, but I eventually checked each book in the mythology section. Not one contained information about a Soul Stealer. I piled the books into neat stacks in front of the shelves. The librarian would likely want them back in their proper places, but my mind was still mulling over the encounter.

"Let's look at what I know," I said, pacing. "He's known as Soul Stealer, so he probably has another name. If we take the name literally, he's stealing souls, but whose, and why? The crows that surround him? Or the people who go missing?" I shook my head. "No, that can't be right. Where would he put all those people?"

I replayed the scene of him pointing his finger. He'd expected something to happen to me, but it hadn't. Was it because it was a dream, or was it because of the burden he spoke about?

"He knew there was something about me. A burden... maybe

the dreams. But then what is his burden?" I sighed. "Kitty, I have far too many questions and not enough answers."

I walked over to a window. It overlooked the village square, now covered with a thick layer of snow. I could see that the snow had also built up under the window as it continued to fall lightly.

"Definitely not going anywhere at the moment."

Candle in hand, I walked around the main room again, then ventured up a metal spiral staircase. My steps broke the silence of the library. The books on the upper level appeared to be mainly stories made up to entertain. Nothing appealed to me, so I carefully descended the staircase.

My gaze fell on a door. Two large iron hinges held its wooden panels in place. The blacksmith had taken the time to mark tiny bookshelves into the metal.

A faded sign hung above the door, nowhere near as grand as the door itself: Restricted Collection.

"Guess there's no one to tell me off," I mumbled.

I turned the handle and pushed with my shoulder. The door creaked open, revealing a room with more shelves and many more books. At a glance, I knew these were far older than the ones in the main room. The old leather bindings cracked, and the gold letters missing from many of the spines.

I crossed my fingers as I stepped over the threshold into a restricted collection room for the first time. Raising my candle,

I saw little blue crystals in the corners of the shelves and on the long table that sat in the middle of the room.

"Oh, I've heard of these," I said, approaching the one closest to me on the table. My hand trembled as I picked it up; it felt cold in my palm. "From the Lasmire Mountains. They really are as pretty as the pictures."

I cradled the crystal into the candle flame. It slowly lit up, casting a bright blue light over my hand. Placing that one back on the table, I repeated the process with the others before blowing out the candle flame. The crystals illuminated the room as if the sun were shining.

I took some time perusing the titles, my fingers caressing the shelves as I read the spines. I rubbed my fingers together; the last shelf had a layer of dust not present on the others.

"Why wouldn't this shelf be as cared for?" I mused. I glanced over the nearby shelves, but they appeared dust-free. "Why are these shelves not as important? Especially in this room?"

I tugged a couple of books free from their tight spaces on the shelf. Their covers were less dusty thanks to how tightly they'd been packed. A musty odour emanated from them, making me crinkle my nose.

"These are a history book and a language book. Odd. This room has fairly ordered shelves, so why are these different?"

I took the books to the table and opened the covers, finding the pages yellowed and foxed with age. On the back of the title page, I saw the place of printing: Grimwood.

"Grimwood, I know that name." I opened the other book. It, too, had been printed in Grimwood. After checking several others, the common theme was the place of printing, even though the printers varied.

I picked up one of the blue crystals and returned to the main room. The kitten remained curled up asleep on the chair. I took the fire poker and nudged at the log. The embers flared, and the flames grew once more.

I walked over to the history section, but there were no books on Grimwood. Still, the name echoed in my mind.

"No books," I said, tapping my finger on a shelf, "but something maybe from school?"

I closed my eyes. The book had said people like me could see the past. Perhaps I could, if I concentrated enough. I focused on clearing everything except the word "Grimwood" from my mind.

At first, all I saw was darkness, but slowly an image faded in, then movement. The schoolhouse stood off to the side, its posts painted blue. I knew they'd been painted green two years prior, but had been blue when I was little. Several children played with a skipping rope on the hard ground nearby. A boy and a girl each held a rope end, and a little girl with red hair skipped as the rope turned.

I stepped closer. Muffled voices became clearer, and then I heard the words the little girl sang as she skipped:

"In Grimwood village, once so bright,
The sun shone down with golden light,
But then the evil came one day,
And all the people faded away.

Now Grimwood stands so very still,
No sounds of laughter, no one's will,
Only the crows that roam around,
Are there to make a haunting sound.

They caw and flap their wings so wide,
And through the streets they smoothly glide,
They perch on trees, on roofs, on walls,
And watch the village as it falls.

For Grimwood now is lost to all,
A place where evil held its thrall,
But listen and hear the pleas,
Hear those whispers on the breeze.

The crows they say, 'Beware, take care,
For evil still is lurking there,
Stay away from Grimwood's gate
Or suffer such a terrible fate.'

So children, heed the crows' advice,
I ask you please to pause, think twice
For though it may seem a game,
The danger there is not so tame."

The little girl jumped from the rope just in time to see Mr Travard standing nearby, scowling in his clean and freshly pressed suit. His hand rested on his hip, with his other raised, one finger about to wag at them.

"How many times do I need to remind you all?" he said. "We do not sing that rhyme!"

Red, wavy hair flew as the little girl turned. I recognised myself.

"But Mr Travard," little Larissa whined, "it's just a song."

"It's not just a song. That is never just a song! Do you want to lure that evil here as well? That's what they say, that the evil hears those words and seeks those singing them. Enough with all this, back inside and practise your adding."

I couldn't discern any features of the other two children, and I had no memory of the scene. Clearly, though, it was the past because I was there.

As little Larissa reached Mr Travard, he caught her arm and leaned down close to her face.

"Stop bringing your dreams to school. No more," he hissed. "I warned your father last week I wouldn't stand for much more of this nonsense. Now get inside."

The frightened girl ran as soon as her arm was free, disappearing into the schoolhouse.

I opened my eyes. The room was the same as a moment ago, but more questions raced through my mind.

"I don't remember any of that," I whispered, "and Papa was still alive then."

I went to the librarian's desk and sat down. From the top drawer, I pulled more sheets of paper and reached for a pencil. The words of the chant echoed in my mind as I wrote them down.

"It must be a real place," I mused, "but not one people talk about. At the same time, they keep the books just away from view."

A bundle of fluff tumbled into my foot.

"Oh, you're awake again?" I picked her up. "I really need to give you a name. 'Kitty' is fine, but I think I can come up with one that suits you more."

She used her claws to climb up my skirt and onto my lap, purred as I patted her back. She nudged my hand, giving me a tickle under my chin. When I stopped giving her attention, she let out a meow.

"You're so pretty," I murmured. "You have an 'M' on your forehead; the fur is so much darker there. Hmm, and you're all shades of grey, like mist. 'Mist'… what do you think of that name?"

Meow.

"Mist."

Meow.

"You like that, huh?"

Meow.

"That's settled then. Now, Mist," I said, stroking her soft fur, "I need to find out what happened to Grimwood, even though there aren't many books about it."

Mist leaped from my lap and padded over to the fireplace. The light from the fire gave her an orange tinge as she groomed herself.

I pushed myself up from the table, wanting to continue researching, but also aware that keeping the fire burning all night might leave me in the cold if the snowstorm settled in for several days.

"Come on, Mist," I said. "Let's put out this fire and see what beds we can find upstairs."

That night, I slept through the sounds of snow falling outside, snuggled in a bed I found upstairs. Mist curled up beside me on the pillow, and no dreams interrupted my rest.

When I woke the next morning, I gazed out the bedroom window. The town centre shone white as the sun lit the scene, though it offered little warmth. A light snow continued to fall, adding to the blanket outside.

Once downstairs, I grabbed more bread and meat from my bag. Mist took off with her piece, batting it around the room before disappearing under a low cupboard. I ate my breakfast, then returned to the room with the restricted books.

"Why not hide them all?" I murmured to myself. The thought had been nagging at me. If Grimwood was being erased from people's memories, why have some books on display and then neglect them?

I leaned on the table, staring at the shelf. The two books I'd removed the day before lay beside my hand. I tapped my fingers on the wood.

"Papa always said to be thorough."

I began moving the rest of the books, two at a time, from the shelf to the table. The dust marked out where they had rested. After removing the last two, I wiped my dusty fingers on my skirt.

I tilted my head, staring at the bare shelf. My gaze flicked to the surrounding shelves before returning to the dust.

"Something isn't the same."

My fingers traced the dust-free space where the books had been. I reached to the back of the shelf, pressing my hands against the wood. I heard a click. The wooden panel fell forward, revealing a metal ring attached to a chain that disappeared into a hole behind the bookcase.

"What's the worst that could happen?" I mumbled. "Spiders, rats… discover a fire-breathing dragon…" With that thought, I tightened my fingers on the ring and pulled.

The bookcase bumped my foot as it creaked open. I released the ring, and it clanged against the wood as it swung from the shelf.

I stepped to the side and peered around the bookcase. Another room with bookshelves awaited. I reached behind me and grabbed a crystal from the table. It lit the way as I stepped around the bookcase and into the room.

There were shelves on every wall, no windows or even a painting. Despite the Grimwood books in the other room looking abandoned, these books were dust-free and resembled those in the main library.

I found four more crystals in the room, giving each a shake to activate their light. Then I began examining the titles, one shelf at a time. I found books on history, legends, food, and people. The one thing they all had in common was the publishing place: Grimwood.

A bundle of grey fur slid past my feet. Mist snatched up a ball of yarn she'd found somewhere, then flipped onto her back and gave it a series of kicks. Soon, the ball came free, and she sprinted after it, disappearing from view as she pursued her foe.

With a smile, I continued perusing the titles, eventually taking three books from the shelves. I sat down at the table and opened them. Two were from the folklore section, and the other was from history. I'd noticed the history book had a different binding and printing style, but looked at the folklore ones first.

The first book was larger than the others, at least the size of three normal books combined. The leather cover was worn, and the letters partially erased. Still, the title remained clear on the first page: *Magical Myths: Where They Began and Their Fate in Time*.

Wind whistled outside. For a moment, I raised my face to the ceiling, noticing the cooler temperature in the room. I hugged myself, wishing I'd brought my shawl. But I wanted to look at the book first.

I turned the crisp page and ran my finger down the list of myths, which were alphabetised. I turned two more pages and found the name I sought: Soul Stealer. I noted the page number and quickly found the entry. My elation dispersed when I realised the text was in another dialect, and I could only understand a few words.

I returned to the main room to retrieve paper and pencils and to work out a plan to decode the information.

"If that page is all there is," I muttered, "I need to know what it says. Time to study the books."

I closed the drawer of the librarian's desk and, after a last look at the snow through the window, walked towards the back room. School was a distant memory—one I'd rather have stayed that way. I sighed at the thought.

The books awaited me on the table, the largest one open to the Soul Stealer page. I checked the other myth book, which had been printed many years before the larger one. There was no mention of a Soul Stealer in it.

I turned to the history book, opening to the front page. The date printed was close to that of the larger myth book.

Grimwood: The Village Lost. Under the title, a portion of the skipping rhyme appeared:

"In Grimwood village, once so bright,
The sun shone down with golden light,
But then the evil came one day,
And all the people faded away."

Despite the mention of the poem, all I found were chapters about the early settlers, the farming successes, the businesses that supported the town, and a few events that were as far from evil as could be.

I eyed the open page on the Soul Stealer. The information there seemed to be my only hope. I looked over the page again, creases forming on my forehead.

"Really?" I grumbled. "Couldn't they have just used a more standard language? No wonder Grimwood isn't talked about in the real world. What I need to do is translate it. Time to stop avoiding it."

My focus fell on a shelf near the entrance of the room. All the books on it seemed to relate to languages, most of which were unknown to me. I chose a book that had symbols with corresponding words in my language. A dictionary; just what I needed. I sat back down at the table.

The pages were crisp as I flipped through the book. I could understand some of the shorter passages that appeared in my language, but even after reading the first page a dozen times, my mind struggled to apply it to the text in the large book.

Two more similar books yielded similar results. I pulled several more from the shelf, then sat down with a thin book I had to pry free from the leather-bound ones that concealed it. I flipped through a few pages and saw the simple format, with the word and its meaning.

"Definitely not as complicated as that other one," I said with a sigh of relief.

I worked through the pages about soul stealers, translating any unknown words. Some sentences made sense, but others were gibberish. Still, as I leaned back in the chair, I read over what I had translated.

"Like dreamers, there is more than one soul stealer." I thought about that for a moment. "He's not *the* soul stealer, just *a* soul stealer. So why am I seeing him? What connects us?"

The book didn't offer an answer. I looked once more at the sketch of a dark, shadowy figure devoid of details, then flipped through the pages. My finger stopped the back cover from closing. On the back page, someone had written:

Beware the dark force that lurks in the night,
It seeks to take your soul and steal your light,
With promises of power and eternal life,
It preys upon your fear, your pain, your strife.

But know that immortality comes at a price,
And the darkness will demand a sacrifice,
Your soul will be its prize, forever to behold,
So choose your path wisely, for your fate is told.

**Even the purest heart can be consumed
by the darkness of fear, and turn from good to evil.**

A village, a neat little village with houses decorated with pot plants and banners. Larissa walked along the cobblestone road and further into the village.

People went in and out of houses. A cat chased a dog around a hay bale, somewhere a rooster crowed, showing he had zero sense of the time of day. With each step Larissa looked for an indication of where she was: a sign, a conversation, anything at all. But while she saw people and could hear chatter, nothing reached her that was clear enough to understand.

Ahead, a lady with her shawl over her hair walked to a building. The lady paused briefly to nudge the fabric to reveal greying hair twisted up into a high bun before she entered the building. Larissa followed her. A sign hung on the building, but the smudged letters were impossible to read.

Inside the building, she watched the old lady approach a man. He was middle-aged, with a neat moustache and a trimmed beard. Spectacles balanced on his nose as he nodded in response to the lady's words. He wiped his hands on a black stained cloth despite the tan-coloured apron he wore covered in similar marks.

"Why can't I hear anything?" Larissa asked. Neither the man nor the lady reacted.

The large cast-iron frame of a printing press sat to one side. A pile of paper sheets sat on a nearby cupboard. Larissa had seen a similar press at Madden's, a local shop that made little cards and sometimes printed stories and news when the weather slowed anything coming from the big cities. *Still, this press is larger than the one back home.*

The lady passed by Larissa and exited the building. Behind the counter, the man watched the door until well after the woman had gone before he returned to the press. He grabbed a sheet of paper and lined it up.

As interested as Larissa was in watching the press, she felt compelled to follow the lady.

Outside, the people nodded and smiled at the lady, who responded in kind. She walked through the village and into the town square. There was no fountain there, but a marble statue of a distinguished-looking man stood tall, surveying all around him.

The lady didn't stop to admire it, though. She continued through the square and moved gracefully through the streets. Soon Larissa saw a large manor house ahead. The many windows dotted at least three storeys.

The lady wasn't even at the front door before servants appeared and fussed over her. One maid took her shawl, another offered her a glass of water. Ushered into the house, the lady paused before a man who stood to one side. He seemed older than the other servants; a tall, imposing man with little hair on his head. Without a word spoken to him, he appeared to know what he needed to do and opened the door for the lady. She smiled and passed by a large mirror that hung on the wall before she entered the room.

Larissa didn't pause to look her reflection and stood at the open door. Another man was in the room and he and the lady chatted away as they sat on comfortable fabric seats. On the wall behind them Larissa saw a painting, the face familiar.

She avoided crossing in front of the people, but moved until the painting hung before her. A young man dressed in a black suit. He stood stiffly and with no expressions of joy or sorrow. Larissa noticed his warm brown eyes, but as she watched, they darkened until they were black.

It was then Larissa raised her hands. They weren't hers. White gloves covered the fingers, but the hands were not small like hers, they were wider and longer.

She turned and ran across the room to look at her reflection in the mirror. As she reached the door, she saw the entrance hall had changed. The polished floors were burnt, the paintings were nothing more than smeared colours where the canvas remained; the walls blackened.

When Larissa breathed in, all she smelt was burnt wood and when she turned around, she saw the mirror on the ground; its shattered glass melted into the floorboards.

Four days I stayed in the library. I found more food in a kitchen at the back, enough to keep both Mist and me from worrying about going hungry.

Every time I remembered a detail from a dream, I wrote it down. I still hadn't worked out who the older woman in the dream was, but I felt she was connected to the soul stealer, though how, I couldn't say.

With the snow still falling outside, I made the most of the library's resources. In the Grimwood collection, I'd found a map of the town and a larger map showing its location. Seeing how close it was to home unsettled me. I'd presumed Grimwood would be as far away as the big cities, yet I knew if the weather cooperated, I might reach it within a couple of days. All I needed was for the snow to stop.

The fire burned warmly that evening. I held a book of myths, reading through different pages. I'd made copies of the entries on dreamers and soul stealers, as well as my translated version from the Grimwood book. The books offered no further information, so I simply browsed.

Mist chose that moment, as I went to turn the page, to spring onto the chair. Tiny claws extended, sinking into the fabric—and my flesh.

"Yelp!" The book tumbled to the floor with a thud.

Meow. Mist retracted her claws and looked up at me with wide eyes.

"Next time," I said, trying to sound stern but failing as a smile crept onto my face, "warn me?"

Meow.

Mist had been good company through the long days and frosty nights. A happy purr rumbled as I ran my hand over her head and down her back.

"Let's hope the book is okay."

I reached down to retrieve the book. It had landed pages down. As I picked it up, I cringed at the sight of the creased pages, smoothing them to restore them.

"Look, Mist," I said, "it's about cats, this one."

Mist clambered up onto my lap and sniffed at the book.

"Who would have thought there would be an entry about cats?" I asked. "Do you want to hear it?"

Meow.

"Some cats are believed to possess the ability to sense evil in creatures such as rats, crows, wolves, and snakes." I paused. "It should be noted that most stories passed down through generations feature crows most prominently. One such recorded legend tells of a great war between cats and crows. The cats had not been bothered by the crows when they first met, but as they observed the creatures, they became convinced that some crows harboured evil powers that could be used against humans. Cats, having always been treated well by humans, made the commitment to protect them against any threat the crows might pose.

The cats discovered certain crows possessed a dark magic that could corrupt even the purest of human souls. These crows would prey on the pain and fears of a human to turn their soul as dark as their own. It is said that when a crow with malevolent intentions entered a village, the cats would immediately know. Their senses became heightened, and they would prowl around, searching for the source of the darkness.

Once the cats located the crow, they would confront it with their piercing stares and sharp claws, determined to drive it out of the village before it could capture a human. The crows, knowing the cats' reputation for sensing evil, would often flee before the cats could even reach them.

Over time, some crows kept their malevolent intentions in check, lest they attract the attention of the watchful feline guardians. The cats and crows reached a fragile truce, but the myth persisted. Cats became known as the protectors of their villages, revered for their ability to keep the darkness at bay. Many humans would keep a cat or two, believing they would sense and protect them from malevolent creatures."

Meow.

"Is that why you found me?" I asked, tickling Mist under her chin. "My little kitty is going to protect me from harm?"

Mist rubbed her head against my hand and snuggled down into the fabric of my dress. Her purrs filled the room.

"My mother must be worried sick," I whispered, closing the book and placing it on the table. "I hadn't intended to be gone so long."

Mist didn't reply; her eyes were already closed. I stroked her soft fur and watched the flames dance for a while. Unlike Mist, I wasn't tired enough to sleep.

Eventually, I reached for the pages of notes under the book, giving them a few shakes to free them. Besides, the general description of soul stealers—which didn't tell me much about the one I'd seen—I'd found a page in the appendix of the myths book with an incantation to take a soul stealer's power.

The incantation echoed in my mind, and I flipped to the page where I had written it down. At the top of the page was a list of ingredients I needed to collect, preferably as many as possible, before reaching Grimwood. Plants like ironbark, pearl petals, and yarrow root could be found in most forests in the area. The pink water I would need to get from the lake about halfway between Willowmist and Grimwood. A crow feather was the last item needed, and any old feather wouldn't do. I needed a feather from the soul stealer I'd seen.

"I wonder if he spends some of his time as a crow?" I mused, stroking Mist. "Perhaps the crows aren't crows at all, but the missing people." I pondered that idea. "If that was true, and he's collecting the crows... how does he steal their souls? I assume that's what he's doing, that he captures them and somehow needs their souls. Mist, it's all very vague."

The kitten turned her head slightly, eliciting a tickle under her chin. She rolled onto her back, remaining asleep with her four little paws in the air. I rubbed her tummy, and a purr rumbled through her tiny body.

I returned the papers to the table. No dream had come to me the previous night, but I felt the pull of one now. I closed my eyes, focusing on the place from my dream with the older lady. My earlier success in putting myself into a dream had proven difficult to replicate. I managed glimpses—the same village, the house before it looked burnt—but staying anchored in the dream long enough proved impossible.

For now, however, I remained in the library, waiting for the snow to stop so I could journey to Grimwood.

The day to leave arrived two sleeps later. I woke to sunlight streaming through the window. Mist rolled back and forth on the floor, basking in the yellow glow where the light touched. The moment I tossed the blankets aside, I could feel the chill in the air was gone.

"Today's the day, Mist," I said. "Ready to venture into the snowy unknown?"

The kitten righted herself and padded over to me, sitting with wide eyes and gazing up as if speaking to me.

"Yeah, I know," I said, stroking her soft fur, "it's nice and cosy here, but I have to help. Are you willing?"

Meow.

With my bag filled with supplies from the library, I placed a note on the librarian's desk, hoping she would forgive me for taking food from the kitchen if I released her from her captor.

I poked at the ashes in the fireplace one last time, wanting to be sure the fire wouldn't rekindle while the library was empty. After checking and double-checking everything, the time had come to leave.

"Ready, Mist?" I asked.

The kitten eyed the door, not looking keen to venture outside, even though the snow had stopped falling. She didn't run when I scooped her up and tucked her into a lightweight, but warm, blanket I had tied like mothers carried their babies. Mist snuggled against me before poking her head out the top.

With Mist watching on, I yanked on the door. It took several pulls before it came free and swung open. A small amount of snow sat near the threshold, but thankfully, the veranda and neighbouring building appeared to have prevented a large drift from forming across the front of the library.

My shoes sank into the snow. They resisted the cold and damp as I stepped through the snow toward the fountain in the square. The depth varied, and I tried to keep an eye out for glimpses of cobblestones.

Soon, Willowmist Pass was behind me. From the map, I knew I needed to follow the main trade road, which passed by Endmere Forest. It would take until about noon to reach it. I hadn't been there before but hoped I could find somewhere to rest that night, as I'd grown accustomed to over the past week.

The further I walked, the easier it became. Winter, it seemed, hadn't quite reached this area yet. I paused several times that morning so Mist and I could eat and take care of business. By the time the sun was high above us, the forest was in sight.

Stories other children told at school surfaced in my mind. Mostly tales of strange creatures and ghosts, though I remembered one Katie had told about a tree coming to life to protect the others from being cut down by a village. Mr Travard, ever the strict teacher who disliked anything magical, had not been impressed. But children continued to tell the stories; they just had a lookout to avoid being caught.

Mist wiggled in the carrier and poked her head up. She'd spent most of the day sleeping but insisted with a meow that the time had come for some proper exploration. Her paws reached for the top of the blanket as her back legs kicked and claws extended to grip the fabric.

"Hang on, Mist," I said. "You want to get down?"

I missed catching her. She got her back legs up and leaped to the ground, mostly landing on her feet.

Meow.

"If you'd waited ten seconds, I could have placed you on the ground."

Mist didn't respond, too busy chasing a butterfly that tried to hide in the low grass near the base of a tree. With a leap, she narrowly missed head-butting the trunk as the butterfly flew to safety.

"Oh, look, some pearl petals," I said. "I'll collect a few."

I bent down as Mist rubbed against my leg. The petals were white, but when tipped to the side, they shone with blues and pinks. I stashed a few away, then turned back to the kitten.

"Come on, Mist," I said, "we need to go as far as we can before dark."

She obliged, running just ahead of me as I walked. My now wet shoes left a muddy trail as we headed deeper into the woods. The trees sheltered us from the wind, and even the air didn't feel as cold.

With Mist continuing to pounce at anything that moved, we walked deeper into the forest. The later it got, the harder it was to decide which way to go.

"Mist, come here, kitty," I called.

The grey bundle of fluff bounded out from a bush and into my hand. I cuddled her for a moment before slipping her into the bottom of the blanket. I felt her pressing against me and felt comforted.

The feeling didn't last. With every step, a wave of unease washed over me. The birds no longer chirped. Every time my shoe crushed a twig, my heart skipped a beat.

Movement. I froze. My heart pounded. The hem of my skirt brushed against my ankles.

"H-hello?" My gaze darted from tree to tree, shadow to shadow. "Stay quiet, Mist."

The kitten uttered a tiny meow and snuggled deeper into the blanket as I turned. Chills ran up and down my spine despite my layers of clothing.

"Make yourself known."

I turned again. Darkness shrouded everywhere I looked. My ears twitched. Something out there had moved.

I took another step. The noise continued. No, not steps, more of a scuttling.

"We need to find shelter, Mist," I whispered. "Something with a lock."

Whatever lurked moved again. I wanted to run, but my feet refused to obey. Again, my gaze darted from bush to tree, but the darkness hid whatever it was. I clenched my hands on the fabric of my dress.

A scream tore through the trees. I shook my leg, trying to rid myself of whatever furry creature was crawling up it. My hands reached down, grabbing the hem of my skirt. I raised it and saw a red caterpillar-type creature on my knee. Its head, with red and yellow markings, rose.

"Ugh, get off you disgusting little…" I swatted it from my knee. It landed nearby, still for a moment, before its head rose again, and its body moved toward me with surprising speed.

Mist meowed at the movement as I, still clutching my skirt, ran. When I finally slowed, checking to make sure the creature wasn't following, I let go of the fabric.

I didn't need to yawn to know I needed rest. But the encounter with the caterpillar had left me with no desire to pause, even to sleep. I continued moving deeper into the forest, hoping to find shelter before my body gave up.

After what felt like hours of travelling through the forest, I finally saw the light of day peeking through the cracks between the trees. My legs ached, and my eyes struggled to adjust to the sunlight after being in pitch blackness for hours. But now that I could see again, I took a moment to rest. I chose an uncomfortable seat on a large rock formation close to the forest's edge.

"I suppose now would be a good time to figure out where to go next," I said to myself, tugging the map from my pocket.

Even with the low temperatures and the snow, I was feeling warm. I studied the map and realised I needed to cross the river that ran past several villages. It wasn't too far from where I sat, but it would be a brisk walk.

When I reached the rushing water, I looked at my reflection in the moonlight. Dark circles underlined my eyes, and my hair stuck out in all directions.

"Oh, dear," I said, "what would Mother say?"

Mist meowed in response.

"No matter," I said. "Let's get past this, then we can rest... somewhere."

Looking down at the current, I saw how quickly it flowed. I wasn't a strong swimmer and was terrified of being swept away. I scanned the riverbank, searching for anything that could act as a bridge.

"Doesn't look like there's a bridge around here," I sighed. "We could spend all night following the river, hoping to find one." I pulled out the map and studied it in the low light. "And there don't seem to be any marked on here, either. We need a plan, Mist."

Meow.

I watched as Mist bounded around in the grass at my feet. I turned and glanced back at the forest. If I used the long grass to tie thicker branches together... maybe I could make a simple, flimsy bridge.

"The best branches would be the ones still attached to the trees," I mused, "and I don't have any tools. I wonder if I could break them with my weight?"

As if she understood, Mist ran to the nearest tree and expertly climbed up to one branch.

"Show off," I grumbled. "I'll probably make a fool of myself. I haven't climbed a tree since I was at school. Oh, well, here goes nothing!"

I took a deep breath, letting it out slowly. My fingers gripped the rough bark as best they could. I braced my foot against a branch, bounced on the other foot, then pushed myself upward.

I pulled myself up a short distance, fingernails digging into the bark. I clung to the trunk, lifting one foot to rest on a branch. A moment later, I got my other foot on a branch. Slowly, I climbed—until my shoe slipped.

The bark peeled away, leaving behind smooth wood. I tried to regain contact with the rough bark.

"No, no, no!" I pleaded in vain.

I landed with a thump on the ground. My breath came in ragged gasps for a moment as I focused on my hand, which lay beside my face.

I sighed, knowing I would have to try again. So I did. Left foot, right foot… Then I almost reached the thickest branches, and… no luck. I slid to the grass again.

Meow.

I raised my gaze to Mist, who sat waiting for me.

"It's definitely harder than you made it look," I said. "One last try."

I climbed the tree again, this time remaining steady as I did so. I was ecstatic when my hand finally gripped the branch. Mist scurried past me and up to the branch above.

Meow.

Looking up, I reached until my hands curled around the branch, then I jumped up and down on the one beneath my feet. I heard a crack and watched as the lower branch fell to the ground.

"One down," I said, "a couple more to go."

Meow.

I climbed down safely, using the branches on the other side of the tree. After repeating the same technique, I had enough branches for a thin bridge. Plenty of vines were available to tie them together. I avoided the poison ones, with their smooth, six-pointed leaves. After tying the last branch, I dragged the makeshift bridge to the river's edge.

Mist scrambled down the tree and joined me as I heaved the branches upright and dropped them across the river. I breathed a sigh of relief when they landed on the other side.

"Come on, Mist," I said. "Let's get going."

With Mist in the blanket, I took several deep breaths. My foot rested lightly on the branches as I made my way across, slowly and carefully. Finally, I stepped onto solid ground.

"I guess that could have been much worse," I said, relieved. "I don't think I can move another step, though. We might need to rest here."

I backed away from the trees. Another rustle of leaves. Had that evil little creature somehow transformed into a human-like figure? Had it caught up with me, looking for a rematch? Laughter pierced the darkness.

"What are you so afraid of?" a male voice questioned. I didn't recognise it.

"Who are you?" I asked, my knees shaking as if the ground itself were moving. My skirt hid my fear from view.

"I mean no harm," the voice reassured me. "This place… it's not the most ideal if you're looking to have a stroll at night."

"I'm not out for a stroll," I replied. "I'm merely looking to set up camp."

As the man stepped out from the shadows of the trees, I could finally make out his appearance. He was tall and slender, with short, unkempt black hair, and he wore simple clothes not unlike what the baker back home wore.

I'd met strangers many times on my journeys between villages, and even during events. While most were friendly and kind, my mother had always warned me to be on my guard. This stranger didn't have clenched fists, he didn't yell, he had made no sudden movements… and yet, I felt a need to be cautious.

"Now that we have that out of the way," he said, "let's try all this again. Set up camp? With what? Now, we know that little bag has a fearsome mouse-catching, bird-chasing killer—"

"She's a very capable companion, I'll have you know."

"—but I must let you know it will hardly keep the creatures away at night."

"Besides," I said, my hand vaguely indicating somewhere behind me, on the other side of the river, "I left my things… just over that way."

"Right, of course. In such a dress, I'm sure you must be highly skilled at camping in the forests."

"Very skilled," I replied. Mist wiggled in the blanket and poked her head up.

"A cat," the man said. "That makes perfect sense. Bring a cat out here to go camping."

"I'm sure you have better places to be than here with me and my cat," I said. Perhaps he would believe Mist could transform into something magical, or at least something larger. Mist meowed quietly. *Not so convincing, kitty.*

"I don't feel right leaving you here alone," he said.

"I don't even know who you are. Or your name."

"I guess that's how things work in polite society," he replied. "A name is fair to share. Call me Draven. What about you?"

"Larissa."

I shifted my weight from one foot to the other, my gaze fixed on him as a smile played on his lips.

"Well, Larissa," he said, "you seem like an intelligent girl, so I'm sure I don't need to bore you with tales about the kinds of creatures that lurk in the woods and hereabouts at night."

"Of course not." My voice trembled slightly as I attempted to bluff.

He hid his mouth behind his hand for a moment, but I heard the chuckle. A hot flush of embarrassment rose in my cheeks. I felt small and vulnerable, like a little girl again, being teased by the girls who could climb trees and swim across the lake. My heart raced as my confidence faltered. I looked down at the ground and took a deep breath.

He might be able to see when I lie, I told myself, *but that doesn't mean I can't still be brave.* I met his gaze once more and straightened my posture.

"Come," I said. "Shall we start with the truth this time? What are you doing out so late?"

"I'm on a mission," I replied.

"What kind of mission?"

"That would be none of your concern." My mother would have approved of the sentiment, even if my tone was harsher than necessary.

"Ah, why must girls be so difficult all the time?" he said with a sigh. "We shall play the game your way, then. But I feel it's best we both leave this place for somewhere more secure."

He turned and started walking. I watched him for a moment, hands on my hips.

"I'm not going to follow you!" I shouted. "You think I would just blindly follow some man who came out of the woods?"

Draven paused and turned, and I saw him shrug.

"If you want to get eaten by a horrific beast, go right ahead," he said. "But I'd suggest you come with me to the camp that's already set up."

"You have a camp?"

"Me and a few others. There's safety in numbers in these woods."

I nodded, but followed a few steps behind, just in case I needed to run. My worries faded when I saw the campfire. The warm orange glow beckoned us into the clearing, where a thick canopy of leaves ensured the snow hadn't touched the ground.

My shoulders relaxed when I saw the other people, some of them my age, some older. Most sat around the fire, and I wanted nothing more than to do the same. Mist wriggled free from the blanket before I could stop her.

"This is a nice camp," I said.

"Thanks," Draven replied. "We do the best we can with what we can find. If there was ever a time for us to work together, it arrived a few days ago."

He gestured for me to sit on one of the fallen tree trunks. Several of the others glanced my way, then turned back to their conversations.

Mist played at my feet as I sat, folding my skirt around my legs for warmth. Draven sat down beside me and offered a bowl of stew. My stomach growled at the delicious smell, and even Mist abandoned her game to jump onto my lap for her share.

"What brought all of you out here?" I asked, picking a piece of meat out of the stew. Mist snatched it and ran off with the meat in her mouth.

Draven sighed, his shoulders slumping forward as he rested his elbows on his knees. His own bowl, already empty, sat at his feet.

"Did you pass through Willowmist on your journey?" he asked.

I nodded, taking another spoonful of the warming stew.

75

"Those of us here…" He paused. "We're the only ones left. It all happened so fast. That night… It was like every other night, except we had the festival in the square, like we do once a month. My dad had asked me to fetch the extra wagon of wood he'd left in his shed on the edge of the forest." He paused again. "That couple over there, they were returning home from visiting family a town over. Those over there had gone on a nighttime rabbit hunt. Each of us here, for whatever reason, wasn't in the square."

"What happened?" I asked, though I already knew the answer. I finished the last of the stew and placed the bowl beside Draven's.

"I had just reached the wagon when I heard the crow calls," he said. "Birds, right? Nothing unusual about birds. Except there were so many. Like a swarm of angry bees, except they had claws and beaks. Straight to the square they went."

"At first, I ran for the square," he continued, "but then I saw this creature in black. Not a crow, some kind of human… thing. I hid. I wasn't brave enough to charge at the thing like others in the square. I hid behind a building and watched as the birds rose and filled the sky. That's when I ran—into the forest, where it was harder for them to see. And then… everything was quiet. We've been here ever since."

"I'm so sorry," I said. "What happened there… it sounds terrible." I hesitated. "Why not return, though? Surely it would be safer to go back to the houses?"

"Maybe," he replied. "Maybe not. Bravery and stupidity: my dad always said they were the same thing, depending on how things turn out."

I smiled. "My dad used to say something similar."

"Was there anything left in the town?" he asked.

I turned to look at him. By firelight, he didn't look menacing, like he had in the forest. Now, he seemed like someone I might meet in town, at Katie's tea shop.

"It was quiet," I said. "Very quiet. I think you would be safe to return, especially with the snowstorms coming through. Being caught out here without shelter... that would probably be more dangerous than hiding in the town."

A young girl threw a handful of branches onto the fire. It flared up, and she danced, a smile on her face. I didn't join in with the clapping and dancing, as a few others did.

Such joy they can feel, I thought, *when surrounded by sorrow and holding onto hope.*

When the revelry quietened, and everyone had settled in to sleep, I lay awake. It wasn't the noises of the woods, or the creatures they concealed, that kept me up. I was afraid the faces of the people I'd just met would merge into a dream, and I'd see them suffering at the hands of the soul stealer.

Sleep eventually won, and I rested... for a while, at least.

Courage isn't the absence of fear,
it's the willingness to face it and try anyway.

The darkness faded away and Larissa found herself in a dark, freezing cold room. Her nose flinched at the musty smell that surrounded her. The furniture in the room stood idle, marked from years without care. She could imagine how grand the room had once been.

On first glance, Larissa hadn't seen the crouched black figure in front of the unlit fireplace. He looked like a piece of furniture covered with a cloth.

"You again? Why won't you leave me be?" he said.

The words were soft, not forceful or confident, like in the square. He stood, though kept his back towards her.

"Dream walkers. That must be the burden you carry. Tell me, are you trying to save me, or destroy me?"

"I don't think I get to make that choice," Larissa replied. Her gaze darted around the room.

"Choices. Choices are a dangerous thing, wouldn't you agree?"

"We make choices to learn, to grow."

"We make choices to get what we want, or at least, we make choices hoping to get what we want."

"Do you have what you want?" Larissa asked.

"No, and yes. I have what I chose to have, but not necessarily what I wanted."

"Why are you taking the people?"

His back straightened. "I don't take people; they grow feathers and fly. They chose to leave, they chose not to stay."

"Perhaps it's not their choice if their will is altered."

"No one's will is truly their own. We are just led to believe that."

Larissa took a step closer, though half the room still separated them.

"Who are you?"

"I told you, I am Soul Stealer. I come, I gift wings, I live on. What about you? Who is it that can join me in my world when she is not near me?"

She hesitated. Her father had claimed that names were important. It was part of who made you, you. Yet, her name didn't define her. Had she another name, she knew she would still be the same person.

"Larissa."

"Larissa, a dream walker. The burden of seeing the past,

present, and future," he paused. He turned so that he faced her. "Tell me, Larissa, what do you see about my future? Who wins?"

"Must there be a winner and a loser?" Larissa countered.

A smile spread across his face.

"Always. There are no prizes for participation, no glory. People remember those that win, those that lose fade away over time."

"Who were you before you were a soul stealer?"

"Ah, so you know there are more who can do what I can then? You have been busy. Perhaps I should have destroyed buildings to ensure that you couldn't learn more about us all. Then again, it's not much fun when the hunter holds all the answers."

He stepped towards Larissa and she countered the move.

"Fear. Courage. Both severely overrated. It is survival, Larissa. Survival is key no matter what; or so I was once told. I was just Eldric then, just a man of flesh and blood, and now I am so much more."

"You must stop what you are doing. Let the people go."

"Do you foresee my downfall, Larissa? Is that why you are haunting me? It's too late to save my soul. I made my choice. If you want me to stop, then you will need to do that."

"I will then!"

His laughter echoed around the room and for a moment, the

features that were unclear became visible. The room appeared as it might have once been.

"You haven't learnt enough, Larissa. It's not a dream walker's role to stop the things they see. They are lessons for you to learn, not to avoid from being."

"Why would I trust anything you would say?"

"Because the soul of a gifted is prized and if you give me the choice, I will take that soul for myself. The reward is too tempting."

He raised his arms. Feather burst from his clothes. Larissa watched on as he rapidly moved towards her. She turned. Stumbled. Got back up and ran for the door. Her hand reached out for the handle when something soft brushed against her hand…

As morning sunlight peeked through the trees, I opened my eyes, taking a few moments to adjust. Mist nudged my hand again.

The memory lingered even as I stretched my stiff limbs. A faint ache in my back and neck reminded me of the hard ground I'd slept on.

Nearby, I heard voices. I turned to find the source and saw the girl who had danced beside the fire talking with an older lady.

I pulled several leaves from my hair. My clothes were rumpled from sleep, but Draven had been right—the trees had provided enough cover to prevent the snow from burying us. A few puddles nearby showed some flakes had snuck through the canopy.

"Never seen anyone so still when they sleep," Draven said.

My cheeks flushed. I hadn't noticed him sitting nearby on a fallen trunk.

"I don't tend to watch people sleep," I replied.

"Still, you were like you were frozen. Some people talk in their sleep, my sister walks in hers, and the old man down the road once threw a jar through his window while fast asleep."

"I guess I get enough movement during the day," I said.

"And yet you look tired, not refreshed," he observed, holding out a plate with bread. He then placed some meat on the ground, which Mist devoured with gusto.

"My body may rest, but my mind does not."

"Nightmares?"

I shook my head.

"Not nightmares, not dreams. Visions. Sometimes of things happening now, sometimes of things that haven't happened yet." I paused.

"Is that how you ended up so close to Willowmist? You saw something?"

I nodded, brushing a stray strand of red hair from my face.

"By the time I made it to Willowmist, everyone was gone. I assume the vision I received was as it happened."

"Why go there then?"

I shrugged. "In case it hadn't happened yet. Perhaps someone would have heeded my warnings, and you all would have been safe."

"And now? You return home to…"

I didn't answer. "I'm going to save the people of Willowmist. They aren't dead, so there's a chance. I'm going to try to make sure he never steals another life."

Draven laughed, then his face sobered. He leaned forward and placed his hand on my knee.

"Wait, you're serious?"

"Yes. I don't know if I'll succeed or fail, but I need to try."

"You? Do you have any idea how dangerous that is? Only a handful of us survived, and that was luck. Had we stumbled, we'd be gone, like everyone else."

"I know, but I need to try. I found some books in the library at Willowmist. I have a plan to reverse the transformation, to turn them back from crows," I said.

"You really shouldn't. And if you do, you shouldn't do it alone," he said.

"I know... but I have to. If I don't, no one will. He'll just keep taking more lives. I have to stop him." I paused. "I never understood why I dreamt like I do. Some say I'm blessed. I think I'm cursed. Maybe... maybe I see things for a reason... Maybe this is why."

"I can't stop you. I would go with you, but I'm needed here." His voice was soft. "You're going to need supplies, and that I can help with."

He watched me, and I wondered what he was thinking. He

finally shook his head and sighed. I watched him move away, collect a bag, and pack food into it.

"Take it," he said, offering the bag.

"What about you? About them?"

"We'll be alright. If this creature has what he wanted, we can go home. We'll be fine. Take it. It's enough for you and the cat for about a week, if you're careful."

My fingers curled around the handle, and he released it.

"If you ever pass back through Willowmist, don't be a stranger," he said.

"I won't. I promise I'll visit."

I shifted my weight from foot to foot, words failing me. Mist was a welcome distraction when her claws grabbed onto my skirt. With a meow, she demanded to be picked up, or threatened to climb.

Draven smiled and took a couple of steps back. He nodded. I turned and headed in the direction I needed to go, despite the pull to stay.

The further I walked, the less I thought about Draven and the others. The sun warmed my arms as I left the forest and entered a meadow. Tiny pink flowers dotted the grass, attracting a swarm of bugs. Mist stalked, leaped, and chased each bee, butterfly, and dragonfly.

The meadow soon fell behind us, and we were once again on a road. Fields of crops replaced the trees. Occasionally, I saw people working amongst them.

"Seems like the Soul Stealer hasn't been this way yet." Mist didn't reply. I patted the pouch gently, suspecting she'd fallen asleep.

The sun crept higher as Mist and I continued our journey. The snow-dusted fields soon gave way to a small town—one I recognised with a jolt. Grimwood.

Its quaint buildings and colourful banners were a stark contrast to the ominous manor looming in the distance. Fragments of my silent vision, following the lady through this very town, flashed through my mind.

"Over there, Mist, in the distance. That's the place from my dream," I said, my voice barely a whisper.

The kitten meowed, looking back and forth. I took a deep breath and continued walking, my gaze flitting from one building to the next.

The printing press shop came into view, its large windows and wooden sign just as I'd seen before. I paused, trailing my fingers along the weathered doorframe as I peered inside. It was empty, the printing press idle, covered in a thin layer of dust. A shiver ran down my spine.

"Nothing here. Like everyone just abandoned the place. Look, the laundry is still on the line." The stained clothing hung stiffly, even the breeze barely moving it.

"Grimwood. The books were hidden away. I wonder if this was the first place the Soul Stealer came. Wiped out the town before moving on," I murmured, my gaze fixed on the fountain. "Imagine the rumours. Wagon sellers passing through, only to find the town abandoned, no sign of why."

Mist meowed softly, her tail twitching as she surveyed the area. I crouched down and ran my hand over her back, grateful for her company.

"I think we need to go to the big house. That's where the lady went." I checked the items I'd collected. "Still need the feather from the Soul Stealer and some yarrowroot. Might be some over in that garden."

We ventured behind a grocer's shop. Opening a creaky gate, I peered into the yard. Once, it must have flourished with edible plants for sale. Now, the snow-covered garden showed little sign of life.

"Snow's thicker here. Wonder if the warm months ever come?" Mist meowed in response. "You're right, we need to find the yarrowroot. Blue and yellow flower with a black centre."

The kitten bounded off, not into the garden, but along the road, her nose twitching as she sniffed the air. She paused next to a garden box sheltered under the veranda of a house. I looked. There, inside, was a single yarrowroot plant.

"Well done, Mist."

I reached down and plucked the flowers. I had everything but the feather.

"Something odd about that house, don't you think?"

From a distance, it looked like any other house, but something about the way the roofline bent, the way the windows failed to reflect the sunlight... A murder of crows rose from the roof, flying towards the trees.

"He's there. That's his house. I wonder if he knows we're coming?"

Meow.

The grand, multi-story house from my dream stood before us, its massive windows and ornate architecture jarring against the simpler buildings surrounding it. I paused, my eyes sweeping over the structure, a sense of dread building within me.

"This is where I saw the lady," I murmured, my gaze drawn to the large, arched entryway. "And the painting..."

Mist meowed again, her small body tensing. We passed through the iron gates, finding the grounds strangely devoid of snow. The once meticulous path was overgrown with weeds and brambles. I pushed through the rustle of leaves and snapping twigs the only sounds.

The manor, once a grand house of stone and timber, now stood a skeletal ruin. Its facade was a blackened, gaping maw, windows like hollow eyes. The ivy, once adorning the walls, was a twisted, charred husk.

I reached out, my hand ghosting over the blackened stone, tracing the outline of a window that had once offered a view. My heart raced as I stepped towards the door.

"What if… what if I'm not ready?" I whispered, glancing around the silent town. "What if I can't do this?"

Mist meowed softly, pressing against my leg.

"You're right. I have to try," I murmured, my fingers closing around the doorknob.

With a deep breath, I pushed the door open. Hinges creaked in protest. The entryway was just as I remembered, polished floors and ornate mirror now shattered fragments on the ground. I stepped inside, my eyes sweeping over the space, bracing for the Soul Stealer.

Silence, except for the faint sound of Mist's paws on the hardwood floor. A chill raced down my spine. I quickly closed the door, sealing us inside.

"Stay close, Mist," I murmured, my fingers tightening around the strap of the bag Draven had given me.

She meowed and stayed close as we moved into a side room.

My gaze swept over the familiar furnishings, my mind racing, trying to recall the details of my dream.

"The painting should be just ahead," I whispered, my pace quickening.

My breath caught in my throat. There, on the wall, untouched by the fire, was the painting—the stern-faced young man in the black suit, his warm brown eyes now darkened to a lifeless black.

I stared at it, my heart pounding. I reached out, tracing the frame, a chill settling over me.

"It's him. He looks human there," I whispered, studying his features.

Mist meowed softly, her tail twitching as she gazed up at the painting. I glanced down at her, a frown tugging at my lips.

"Keep an eye out for a black feather. His black feather."

She wasn't a dog, but I hoped her nose would lead us to what we needed. I turned away from the painting, ready to move through the house. The lower floors were damaged at the front, but the rear, where the kitchens and servant stairs were, looked untouched.

"Come on, but be super quiet." We crept up the narrow stairs, emerging into a corridor.

One side stood blackened and charred. The other, untouched. We walked towards a set of heavy wooden doors, each with a rose carved into a frame.

"This must be it, Mist," I whispered, brushing my fingers against the cold doorknob.

Meow. Mist crouched, her tail still. I pushed the doors open.

A vast room spread out before me. High ceilings painted with scenes of fields and animals. Bookshelves lined one wall. Chairs stood idle. At the far end, a fireplace rose to the ceiling, obscured by a figure in black, his back to me.

"You again," he said. "I was beginning to wonder if you would ever find your way here."

A chill ran down my spine. I instinctively stepped back, my hand tightening around my bag.

"Soul Stealer," I breathed.

He turned, his dark eyes fixing on me, a slow smile spreading across his lips.

"Larissa," he said, his voice dripping with amusement. "Call me Eldric, though it's been a while since I've heard my name."

Mist let out a low growl, her small body tensing as she positioned herself between us. I felt a surge of pride and gratitude. I reached down to give her a gentle pat.

"What did you do with the people?"

He straightened and gestured to the chairs, but I stayed put.

"What are people? Going about their days, doing the same

94

thing over and over, hoping something might change. They live, they die, they're forgotten. A bit like your father."

"What?"

"You didn't think you could just come here, and what? Demand I do as you ask? You researched me. I did some digging on you, too. Your little town. Your family. I didn't realise we'd crossed paths before."

"I don't understand."

"Dream walking is a family thing. Passed down. A cycle that ends only if there's no child. Your father was a dream walker. I'd quite forgotten about him. Ten years ago, or so?"

"You knew my father?"

"Knew is a strong word. No, I didn't know him, but he came to a town I was collecting from. Put up quite a fight before growing feathers. I even went to the effort of faking a sickness to cover the deaths. Back then, I was more careful. Now, I just don't bother."

"You turn people into crows? Why?"

"Because, Larissa, I made a deal, and when you agree to something, you must follow through, no matter what. It's called an obligation. Your father boosted my count nicely, which is why I'll be pleased to take yours too. A step closer to fulfilling my end."

"What was the deal?"

Eldric sat down in one chair and clicked his fingers. Flames roared to life in the fireplace. I looked down. Mist was gone. I darted my gaze around the room, but she was nowhere to be seen.

"A deal signed in blood. Look at this house, ravaged by fire. Not much survives that. I survived, but I didn't."

"How can that be?"

"You are so young. There are many ways to live and die. The night of the fire, I died. The man in the mirror... no longer me. People cowered and hid. My family worked generations for this place, and bit by bit, it was falling apart. So I struck a deal, got back what I'd lost. The more souls I collect, the more of this place is restored."

"You're taking people for a house? What kind of person does that?"

He looked back at me and smiled. "Someone who is no longer a person, but a blend of things."

"You need to let the people go."

His laughter echoed around the room. "Let them go? Most are already gone. The last few collections are still waiting for delivery."

"What will it take to make you stop?"

"Nothing, my dear. My soul is too invested." He turned back to the fire. "But I don't like leaving guests empty-handed.

Perhaps we can make a deal?"

"Why would I do that?"

"I don't like being followed, in my dreams or here. It's not your role as a dream walker, and it's annoying."

"How could I believe anything you'd agree to?" I asked, my voice trembling. "You're a liar and a monster."

"I kept my word on my other deal. Why would I do any less for you?" He turned to face me again. He stood and took a step towards me, his hand reaching out. "I'm simply making a proposal. Leave me alone, and you can be reunited with your father."

My breath caught in my throat. I stared at him, my mind racing.

"What are you saying?" I whispered.

His smile widened. He took another step closer, reaching out to touch my face.

"I can bring him back, Larissa," he said. "All you have to do is sign an agreement."

Doubt warred with temptation. I leaned towards him, the promise of seeing my father again reeling me in.

Mist suddenly pressed against my leg, scratching her claws across my ankle. I glanced down. Trails of blood. The kitten crouched, back arched, growling at Eldric.

"No," I said, my voice firm. "I won't do it. My father wouldn't want me to, and I won't betray the people you've already hurt."

His expression darkened. He let out a low chuckle, withdrawing his hand.

"Very well, Larissa," he said, his voice dripping with contempt. "If you won't help me willingly, then I'll have to take what I want by force."

With a gesture, the room filled with the flapping of wings. I watched in horror as dozens of crows descended from the shadows, their beady eyes fixed on Mist and me.

Fear surged through me. I reached into my bag, pulling out the items I'd gathered from the library and along the way. I had to act fast.

"Mist, I need one of his feathers," I said.

Meow. She batted a feather towards my foot.

"Good kitty," I said.

The crows circled, their sharp beaks and talons glinting in the dim light.

I took a deep breath, tightening my grip on the objects in my hand. I chanted the words I'd memorised from the ancient tome.

The crows cawed, their wings beating the air as they closed in. As the chant reached its crescendo, power surged through me. I watched as the crows transformed, their black feathers melting away, revealing the terrified faces of the missing villagers.

"No, you can't release them!" Eldric yelled. Black feathers replaced his suit.

Souls danced around the room and vanished from sight. I did not know if they were free or dead. I focused back on Eldric. The chant was for him.

"You can't maintain the transformation. This will strip you of your power," I said.

"This isn't over, Larissa," he growled. "You may have broken my hold, but I still have plans for you."

A chill ran down my spine. I tightened my grip on the objects. I continued chanting as a breeze whipped through the room. The black feather in my hand wrenched free, flying towards Eldric.

"Oh no," I said. "Mist, we need to go."

My heart pounded as I raced through the manor's dimly lit corridors, Mist a blur of grey fur beside me. The objects in my hands, remnants of the spell that freed the villagers, felt heavy.

"We need more time. We weakened him, but for how long?" I said, glancing over my shoulder.

Behind us, the deafening caws of pursuing crows echoed through the halls. I pushed myself harder, following the familiar path toward the grand entryway, desperate to escape and figure out my next move.

Rounding a corner, I skidded to a halt, nearly colliding with a towering figure clad in black. Eldric. His dark eyes glinted with malice, a cruel smile twisting his lips.

"Leaving so soon, Larissa?" he purred. "And here I thought we were just getting acquainted. I'll give you one more chance. One more chance to leave me in peace."

"I can't. I've come too far. You made your deal, and I've made one with myself."

"Then you leave me no choice," he growled, raising his hand.

I tightened my grip on the objects, knuckles turning white. Beside me, Mist growled, hackles raised.

"Back down, Eldric," I growled, forcing confidence into my voice. "You lost those you stole away."

"Not lost, merely delayed. They were freed, but I can just as easily reclaim them. You accomplished nothing."

"No. I'll finish what I started."

He took a step closer, his gaze piercing mine. "You think you can waltz in here and undo years of work? You're a fool."

A chill shot down my spine. "I know exactly what you're doing, Eldric."

"You do not know what's at stake," he said, his voice low and urgent. "You've seen glimpses of my past, perhaps present. I doubt even a dream walker could truly understand how I came to be like this. Besides, even if you strip my powers, another will rise. There is always that want in humans. Wanting what we can't have."

"You set the fire, destroyed your family, didn't you?"

The corner of his mouth curled up. "So naïve. That's the best you could come up with? You're too young to understand my story." He paused, glancing down at Mist. "I detest cats. Predators of birds. Keepers of souls. I don't like you either, furball."

"Leave her alone."

He let out a frustrated sigh, clenching his fists. "Worry about yourself. You've left me no choice. With no feather of mine, you can't complete the spell. Your journey ends here."

With a sudden motion, he raised his hand, fingers curling inward as he unleashed a surge of dark energy. I braced myself, the objects in my hands glowing faintly, my mind repeating the words of the spell.

"It's no use without the feather. You can't destroy what you can not touch or see."

Eldric stepped forward. I was frozen as his fingers tightened around my neck. Mist's desperate cries reached my ears. I saw Eldric flinch in pain.

"You foolish girl," he hissed, his face inches from mine.

I clawed at his hand, my lungs burning, fighting for air. But his grip was relentless, my strength fading.

"Your father was a fool, just like you," he spat. "History repeats itself. Over and over."

A grey blur shot into view. Mist dug her teeth and claws into Eldric's arm, his grip loosening. I pulled away, stumbling back to the ground. I looked up to see him swinging his arm, trying to dislodge Mist.

"You're the one who's a fool, Eldric," I rasped, barely a whisper. "I won't leave this unfinished."

"Darn cat!"

Mist let go and tumbled into the long grass. Eldric checked his sleeve, blood seeping out, the sleeve slowly transforming into feathers.

"The blood and feathers must be connected," I murmured, scanning the ground for a usable feather or drop of blood.

"Time to join your father, Larissa. For it is only in death that you will find peace."

I dropped the objects onto my skirt. He was steps away. A rustle in the leaves. Mist darted out; her mouth filled with black feathers. She raced to me, dodging between Eldric's feet. He kicked out, missed, and lost his balance.

"Forgive me, Eldric," I whispered.

Mist spat the feathers into my lap. I began the chant:

By pact of dark and whispered deal,
Souls were stolen for power's feel,
To pay the price, their fate to seal,
Now break the bond, let wounds reveal.

With moonlit beams and stars that gleam,
I call upon the ancient stream,
Undo the wrong, end wicked dream,
Return to human, pure and clean.

By shadowed night and dawn's first light,
I shatter chains, expose the blight,
Strip the power, end the fight,
Restore their form to human right.

By earth and sky, by sea and flame,
I speak the words, I call your name,
Your power's gone, you're but a frame,
Human once more, the soul's reclaim.

Eldric raised his head, his hand reaching out even as his face contorted. His body convulsed, feathers falling away in piles around him. He was so still, I thought he was dead.

"Eldric?"

I stood, letting the objects fall to the ground. Mist walked beside me as Eldric came into view. His face and hands were no longer the same.

"What happened to you?"

He didn't respond. Reaching out with scarred and twisted hands, he pushed himself up. He turned his face towards me, and I saw the damage. One ear was missing, his eyes barely visible, his skin wrinkled from burns.

I stepped back as he rose. He made no attempt to come closer, walking back into the manor instead. I followed, watching him pick up a broken mirror shard and stare at his reflection.

"I'm sorry," I said.

Another black-clad figure appeared in the doorway. Mist resumed her attack position.

"You've done enough today. I have a contract to collect on."

The doors slammed shut. A scream rose, though I wasn't sure if it was real. Then flickering light danced in the windows as flames tore through the rooms.

I scooped up Mist and fled, watching from Grimwood village as the manor burned until nothing remained but ash.

EPILOGUE

I walked through the familiar streets of my village, Mist padding at my side. As I passed the bustling shops and familiar faces, a wave of relief washed over me. I was home.

Mist meowed softly, her large eyes gazing up at me. I scooped her into my arms, holding the small bundle of fur close.

"Thank you, Mist," I whispered, my voice thick with emotion. "I couldn't have done it without you. Now I just need to work out how to explain all this to Mother."

The kitten purred, nuzzling against my chest.

I reached my family's door and paused, my gaze sweeping over the familiar surroundings. A small smile touched my lips.

"I'm home, Father," I whispered, my fingers tightening around Mist's soft fur. "I only wish you could be here to see it."

With a deep breath, I pushed open the door and stepped into the embrace of my mother's loving arms.

"Oh my, don't do that again, young lady," she said.

"You know where I've been?"

She stepped back. "A young man came to say he saw you. Said you were following your dream. Your father would be proud."

My cheeks grew warm.

"Was it Draven? The one who told you?"

"It was. He's been here several days. I sent him to get some fresh bread, as I knew you'd be here."

"How did you know?" I asked, surprised.

She smiled. "Dream walking is how I met your father. Couldn't keep out of them."

"Why didn't you tell me?"

"I haven't seen much since your father passed. But I saw you returning here, and the way you become lost for words when Draven walks through that door." I turned just in time to see Draven coming down the path towards the front door. "Come on, Mist. I saw you too and have something nice ready."

Draven looked up as he reached the door, a smile spreading across his face.

"Not bad for a dream," he said.

"I was supposed to visit you," I replied, remembering my promise.

"Decided not to leave it to chance."

I stepped aside to let him enter. Souls were valuable, especially when they were connected.